LUCY'S SECRET

REINDEER

Anne Booth

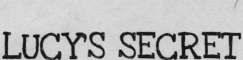

SCHOLASTIC INC.

ISBN 978-1-338-24566-0

12 11 10 9 8 7 6 5 4 3 2 1   17 18 19 20 21 22

Printed in the U.S.A.   40

First Scholastic printing, November 2017

To Mom and Dad
-Patrick and Anne Simms-
who always made Christmas so special

Writing to Santa

School had finished, the Christmas tree was up, and the fairy lights were twinkling. Dad was busy hanging tinsel, paper chains, and Christmas cards in crisscrossing cheerful lines across the room. He had the radio on loudly and was singing along to the Christmas songs. Dad loved the Christmas holidays.

Mom was in the kitchen, making Sunday lunch. Lucy's big brother Oscar was lying on the sofa, playing video games, and Lucy was sitting at the table, writing her letter to Santa.

"There isn't any point in writing to Santa," said eleven-year-old Oscar, who had got bored with his game and was looking over her shoulder. "You're eight, not a baby."

Lucy was just about to get very cross and do something very unChristmassy to her brother when, luckily, Mom stuck her head around the door.

"Oscar, can you help me set the table?" she asked. "And Lucy, can you go and tell Gran that lunch is ready?"

Lucy was glad to go and get Gran, and quickly put on her boots and coat. As she closed the door behind her she could hear Oscar complaining loudly about being made to do all the work while Lucy wrote stupid letters.

Lucy crossed the lane and went down the little garden path to Gran's side door.

"Hello, Gran!" Lucy called, as she pushed the door open and stepped into the kitchen.

At one end of the large room was a big kitchen range and a dresser with

3

pretty patterned plates and cups on. There was also a sink and a cozy armchair with patchwork cushions. But the other end of the room was like a little animal hospital. There was a row of cages for injured or sick animals, and there were shelves stacked high with all sorts of animal food, biscuits, and mealworms. Lucy knew the cat food was for the little hedgehogs Gran found in the winter which were too small to survive the cold and hibernation. On the big wooden kitchen table in the middle of the room was a set of weighing scales, but instead of weighing flour or sugar Gran was weighing a hedgehog.

"Hello, Lucy, darling," Gran said. "Is lunch ready? Just let me write down Brian's weight. I think he's heavy enough to be put out to hibernate soon. He's just over one pound—isn't that great?"

As Gran popped Brian back in with the other little hedgehogs she was feeding up, Lucy checked on the rest of the animals. A little red-breasted robin with an injured wing was hopping around a big cage, and a rabbit with a bandaged paw was asleep in another. As soon as the wild birds and animals got better Gran would set them free, although the very little hedgehogs would stay in the warm with her until spring.

Gran washed her hands and put on her coat to walk over to Lucy's house. They closed the door and left the birds and animals sleeping safe and sound.

Lucy could hear the sound of plates and cutlery being laid out on the dining table when she and Gran arrived. Dad took Gran's coat while she admired the decorations, and then they all went through to the dining room and sat down. Mom had lit some candles and it felt as if Christmas was getting very near. Oscar stopped being grumpy and told Gran all about the football team he wanted to get into and the karate classes he had started. Now that he was in 6th grade, it seemed to Lucy as if he didn't want to come after school and help with Gran's animals any more.

"Mom, please can I have a stamp for my letter to Santa?" Lucy asked, after they'd finished their pudding. "I need to send it today so it gets there in time."

"Only losers write to Santa," muttered Oscar.

"Oscar!' exclaimed Mom, shocked.

"Don't be mean, Oscar," Dad said, looking very hard at him.

"What a strange word to use," Gran said, thoughtfully. "Why do you think Lucy is a loser, Oscar?"

"Writing to Santa's a babyish thing to do," Oscar said, sulkily. "And anyway, it doesn't work. Lucy asked for a horse and she got a rocking horse. Even last year, she didn't get the puppy she asked for."

"Maybe Santa didn't think Lucy was old enough for a puppy last year," Dad said.

"I'm sure he did his best with the presents," Mom said. "Lucy got a very nice pajama-case dog. You love Scruffy, don't you, Lucy?"

"I do love Scruffy, and I'll write to Santa and tell him," Lucy said. "I'll ask him if he needs any help with anything, too."

"What a lovely idea, Lucy," Mom said.

"I'll do the dishes, Emma," Dad said. "And I'll cook the rest of the meals this week—and help with Christmas dinner! It's nice to be home from work and able to help out for a change," he added, getting up from the table.

"That would be the best Christmas present of all," Mom said, and Dad made her smile by holding some mistletoe over her head to get a kiss from her.

"Yuk!" said Oscar and Lucy at the same time, and everyone laughed.

"There's a stamp in the drawer, Lucy," Dad said. "Maybe Gran can go out with you to send your letter to Santa. Oscar, you can bring the dirty dishes into the kitchen with me." Oscar opened his mouth to argue . . .

"I mean it," Dad said, firmly, and Oscar started collecting the plates.

Dreaming
of Kittens

Lucy drew a picture of a reindeer on
her letter to give it a proper Christmassy
look. She gave it to Gran to read before
she put it in the envelope.

Dear Santa

    I would like a kitten for Christmas.
I don't want a horse or a dog in case it
hurts Scruffy or Rocky's feelings. They
think they are real. But please can the
kitten be really real this time? Gran says
to tell you that I have been helping her
all year, and she thinks I am ready for a
pet. This year I have fed the hens, and

the rescue guinea pigs, and the rescue
rabbits. I have helped with the baby
hedgehogs and a fox Gran looked after.

Lots of love from
Lucy

P.S. I know you must be very busy at this
time of year, but I'm on vacation now
and can help you if you need me. Here
are some pictures of the animals I have
looked after this year:

"Lovely!" Gran said, and gave her a hug.

Lucy put the stamp on the envelope and addressed it.

"It isn't only losers who write to Santa," she said to herself. She hoped Santa hadn't heard Oscar. He could be so rude.

Gran took her hand as they walked to the post box, and it made her feel safe and Christmassy again. She closed her eyes and wished very hard as she sent her letter, and she thought she heard the sound of sleigh bells chiming. It made her feel tingly inside. When she opened her eyes something wonderful had happened— snowflakes were falling all around!

Somehow she knew deep down that Santa would get her letter and read it.

"Do you think Santa will ask for my help, Gran?"

"I don't know, Lucy, but I'm sure he appreciates your kind thought. And if he doesn't need you, I certainly do! There are lots of animals who need help at Christmas."

"Gran, do you think Oscar will be all right?" Lucy asked, as they walked back home in a world that was getting whiter and whiter. "He hasn't written a letter at all. What if he doesn't get anything from Santa because he has been so rude?"

"Don't worry, Lucy. I'm sure Santa understands. He knows Oscar has a kind heart really."

Lucy wasn't sure about that. It seemed like a long time since Oscar had done anything kind for her.

Oscar was in a much better mood when they got back, and Gran stayed and they all played Monopoly together. Snow kept falling steadily all afternoon, covering ordinary hedges and walls with white magic. Lucy looked over at Mom and Dad laughing together.

"Dad, can we go sleighing this Christmas?" she asked.

"Yes! I've got a whole week at home

with you—so let's do lots of fun things!"
Dad said.

Gran set off for home just as it was
getting dark. She put so many layers on
Dad teased her that she was as plump as
Father Christmas.

"Grandma Christmas," Oscar said,
and Gran laughed and ruffled his hair.
She was the only one who was allowed
to do that.

"I want a drum kit for Christmas," Oscar said later that night, when he and Lucy were in the bathroom brushing their teeth.

"Have you written a letter to Santa?" Lucy asked.

"Not exactly . . . " Oscar replied. Suddenly he flicked the water from his toothbrush at her and ran off to bed before she could get him back.

When Lucy had finished, she went into her bedroom. "You're going to meet a new friend soon," she told Rocky. "I've asked Santa for a kitten, and I think this year he might think it's the right time." Her rocking horse

rocked back and forth thoughtfully, his eyes kind and brown, his fur gleaming in the moonlight. She could almost hear his soft whinny. He really was a beautiful horse. Scruffy looked up at her from her bed, and she knew that if he could, he would wag his tail. She did love them.

"Sweet dreams, you two," Lucy said as she got into bed and lay down, cuddling Scruffy.

"Sweet dreams, Mom," she said as her mom came in to close her curtains and kiss her goodnight. "I'm going to dream of kittens."

"Why do you say that?" Mom asked. "Have you been talking to Gran again?"

"I've been writing to Santa. I've asked for a kitten and told him how I've helped look after all Gran's animals this year."

"Lucy, love, don't get your hopes up too much, will you?" Mom said, as she

kissed her cheek. "We don't always get
what we want but I'm sure Santa will do
his best."

Dad came in then and sat down on
her bed.

"Sweet dreams, Dad. Hope you dream of kittens," Lucy said. "Then you'll know what Santa is bringing me."

"What color kitten do you want me to dream about?" Dad asked, very seriously.

"I don't mind, as long as it loves me," Lucy said.

"How could any kitten not love you?" Dad chuckled, and ruffled her hair the way Gran did.

"Goodnight, Lucy!"

"Goodnight, Dad!" Lucy replied.

Sleigh Bells

Lucy woke to the sound of sleigh bells, which faded away as she sat up. She rubbed her eyes. It was still night-time, and everything was quiet. "I must have been dreaming," she said to herself, but she felt awake and excited and she didn't know why. She got out of bed and opened the curtains. Outside the window, the snow was falling in white swirls. Inside the room suddenly felt magical, with tiny stars sparkling in the air. As Lucy watched them, the stars formed into letters.

"Look under your pillow, Lucy!" the stars spelled out in front of her.

She turned and saw something white sticking out from under her pillow. She drew it out. It was an envelope addressed to her, and the stamp had a picture of Santa on it. As she looked at it, Santa seemed to wink at her! Lucy blinked, shook her head, and looked again. Santa on the stamp smiled and nodded at her, and then the stamp stayed still again. Dazed, she opened the envelope. The white paper she took out shimmered as she read the big, black, curling handwriting on it:

Dear Lucy

Thank you so much for asking me if I needed help. Nobody does that. What a kind girl you are! As a matter of fact I do need help. My smallest reindeer is not very well and needs someone to nurse him back to health before

Christmas Eve. I know you have helped look after your gran's rescue animals, so I am asking you to do this very important job. Go down to the garden shed and you will find him.

Thank you, Lucy. I am relying on you to help me. I have to have all the reindeer well or I won't be able to deliver the presents. Starlight may be small, but he is a very important part of the Christmas team. He shows us where to go, and without him we'll never find all the children's homes in time.

*But, Lucy, this is TOP SECRET!
That's why this letter will
disappear as soon as you finish
reading it.*

Lots of love from

Santa

Lucy rubbed her eyes to check it wasn't all just a dream, but there they were—the envelope and the letter on her bed, twinkling and glowing.

"Look, Scruffy! Look, Rocky! A real letter from Santa! I have to look after one of his reindeer!" She picked up Scruffy. She could almost feel him wriggling with excitement in her arms. Then there was the sound of sleigh bells again, and the letter, the envelope, and the smiling Santa stamp disappeared, leaving just a cloud of stars that glittered and faded.

"I wish I could have shown that letter to Oscar," Lucy said to Scruffy and Rocky, as she rushed to put on her cozy red slippers and dressing gown. She tiptoed downstairs, her heart thumping, and put on her red duffel coat over her dressing gown. She turned the key in the back door and went out into the garden.

It was beautiful. There was snow on the garden path, and her slippers got a little wet as she crunched along. In the moonlight the snow looked as if it had lots of little diamonds in it, and the sparkling seemed to get brighter the nearer she got to the shed. She pushed the door open . . . But it was just a garden shed, full of boxes, watering cans, and garden tools.

I must have just dreamed it all, Lucy thought, feeling very disappointed. Of course Santa wouldn't write to me. She was just about to pull the door closed again and rush back into the house to get warm when she saw something move. Could it be . . . ? Her heart started beating faster, and she walked right into the shed up to a pile of old flowerpots and peeked over.

What Santa had told her was true! There, in the corner, was a very small reindeer. A beam of moonlight came through the shed window and fell on his soft white fur. Lucy could see him breathing as he looked up at her. This was better than anything she had ever asked for. Ever.

"Hello, Starlight," she whispered. "Don't be frightened. It's Lucy." She tiptoed carefully forward, moving a bucket to the side as she went. The reindeer was only about the size of Rocky—not much bigger than a small dog. He was so little he didn't even have big antlers like the pictures on Christmas cards; just baby ones, peeping through his fluffy coat.

How could you ever help to pull a sleigh? Lucy wondered. She had never been this close to a reindeer. She'd never even seen one in real life before. This was a real, live animal, not a picture or a toy. She put her hand out slowly and felt him reach out his soft muzzle to nudge it. Gran always told her never to rush an animal when you meet it. Starlight's breath was warm but his nose was cold.

He was lying down on his side, his long legs splayed out. His big brown eyes had long eyelashes and he looked bewildered. He shivered a little.

"You're cold," Lucy said anxiously, and edged herself forward so that she could sit cross-legged on some sackcloth next to him. When she felt ill the first thing her mom did was put her in bed and wrap her up so that she was cozy and warm. She looked around for something to wrap him up in. There was an old picnic rug they hadn't used since the summer, an old gardening jacket Dad used sometimes, and more sackcloth.

Starlight's tail wagged a little. It reminded Lucy of the lambs in the fields at springtime. She opened her coat and carefully pulled him up on to her knee, then she tried to snuggle them both under some sackcloth, Dad's jacket, and the rug. At first he was all long legs and baby antlers, and it was a bit tricky sorting out all the layers, but she knew she had to warm him up by cuddling him. Eventually he settled down on her lap. He was surprisingly light and furry, and just holding him in her arms made her think of stars and snowflakes and Christmas bells and the feeling you get when school finishes for the holidays.

"I wish I could take you into school to show everyone," she said, stroking his soft fur. He sniffed and snuffled and gently nuzzled her face and looked deep into her eyes. Then he sighed, tucked his long legs up, and snuggled into her, his hard baby antler buds resting against her chest. It was a bit uncomfortable, but finally she managed to shuffle into a position against the wall. Soon the shed was full of the sound of a baby reindeer snoring.

"I can't believe you're here, Starlight," she said, looking down at the sweetest little reindeer she could ever have imagined. "But what should

I do now?" Starlight just wriggled in his sleep, his ears twitching. He shivered again and Lucy held him tighter to keep him warm. She knew it was up to her to get him well for Christmas.

Keeping a Secret

Lucy must have fallen asleep, because the next thing she knew, a small wet nose was nudging her cold face. As she opened her eyes, she saw two big brown eyes staring back at her. She was sitting on the floor in the garden shed.

The snow-bright daylight was streaming through the window and she had a real-life little Christmas reindeer in her arms. It was all true!

"Hello, Starlight!" she laughed. "You're looking much better!" His little tail was wagging as he climbed off her lap and shook himself. He looked so sweet and small. He even tried to give a little jump! He still wasn't strong enough though, and his legs wobbled and crumpled underneath him. He shivered. Lucy took off her coat and wrapped him up in it to make a sweet little bundle. He didn't wriggle or try to get out of it, but let himself be tucked up snugly again. Lucy put him down carefully on a little nest of sacks, covered him with the rug and Dad's jacket again, and lined up flowerpots around him, partly to hide him and partly to protect him from the draft. He watched her solemnly with his big brown eyes but didn't move.

"I should put up a curtain so nobody can see you through the window," Lucy said. "I promised Santa I'd keep you a secret."

Starlight closed his eyes peacefully.

"Don't you worry about anything, Starlight," Lucy said, beaming at him. "I'm going to get you strong for Christmas. Wait here. I'll be back."

It was cold outside in the snowy garden just wearing her dressing gown, and Lucy was glad to find the kitchen door was still unlocked. The good news was that she could get indoors. The bad news was that she met Mom coming down the stairs.

"Hello, Lucy, love," Mom said, surprised. "What are you doing up so early?"

"I . . . I was a bit hungry. Um . . . do you have a carrot, Mom?"

"A carrot?" Mom laughed. "That's an unusual breakfast!"

"I just really feel like one," Lucy replied.

"There are some in the vegetable rack. Make sure you wash it first. In fact, you may need to peel it," Mom said. "I'll show you how."

This wasn't what Lucy wanted. Starlight was in the shed alone, and here she was, washing and learning to peel a carrot she didn't even want to eat!

"You'll never guess what Lucy is having for breakfast!" Mom said, as Dad and Oscar came downstairs. "A carrot!"

"Rather her than me," Dad said, filling his and Oscar's bowls with cereal. Lucy reluctantly munched her carrot and tried to look like she was enjoying it. While Mom was pouring the tea and Oscar and Dad were laughing over a joke on the back of the cereal packet, Lucy edged her way over to the cupboard and sneaked another carrot out. She thought for a moment that Oscar had seen her, but he just looked away and carried on being silly with Dad. So Starlight's breakfast was sorted. Now to keep him hidden.

"Mom, do we have any spare curtains?" Lucy asked. "I thought . . . I thought I might do a puppet show for Christmas."

"Do you want to make a theater?" Dad said, looking interested. "I'll help! I love a good puppet show."

Oh no, thought Lucy.

"That's not fair!" Oscar said. "I thought you were going to come to the music shop with me and look at drum kits."

"The ones with headphones," Mom said quickly to Dad.

"Oh yes," Dad said. "Sorry, Lucy. Can you wait until we come back? Oscar's seen a drum kit in the music shop and we're going to try to be there when the shop opens."

"Yes, that's fine," Lucy said, relieved, edging her way to the door, a carrot behind her back.

"I think there's an old red velvet curtain folded up at the bottom of my wardrobe," Mom said. "I was planning to make something nice with it but I wasn't sure what, and I've just been too busy to get around to it. You can have it."

Lucy went upstairs, got dressed, and found the curtain. It was perfect. The velvet was a little worn, but it was thick and heavy and nobody would be able to look through the window and see Starlight.

"I'm doing my best, Santa," Lucy said under her breath. "I'll keep the secret and Starlight will be well for Christmas."

She waited until she heard Dad and Oscar go out and then tiptoed down the stairs, the curtain in her arms with the carrot hidden under it.

Mom was in the kitchen. She had her special Christmas apron on and she was making cakes.

"Lucy—here—you can lick the spoon," Mom said. "And once the cakes are cooked we'll decorate them for Christmas. You can make the icing and then we'll put sprinkles on them. It'll be fun!"

"Um . . . I have to make my puppet show," Lucy said.

"There's time for both," Mom said. "It wouldn't be Christmas without us making our cakes together. We have to get a special one ready to leave for Santa tomorrow, like we always do. It's one of my favorite bits of Christmas!"

It was one of Lucy's favorite jobs too. She and Mom always put lots of decorations on the cakes, and leaving out the biggest one for Santa, and carrots for his reindeer, was something they always did every Christmas Eve. But today she really wished she didn't have to do it. She just didn't have time.

"Can I just put the curtain away?" Lucy said. "I want to put it in the shed."

"The shed? You don't have to make your puppet theater in the shed," Mom said, surprised. "It's too cramped and cold and dusty in there."

"I've . . . I've just got some surprises in the shed. For Christmas . . . " Lucy said. "Please don't look."

Mom laughed. "OK, Lucy, I'll stay away from the shed. But if any of those surprises are chocolate, don't keep them out there. I'm pretty certain there are mice. It really would be better to keep your presents in the bottom of your wardrobe. No one would look, I promise."

But Lucy was out of the back door before her mom could stop her. "I'll be back in a few minutes," she called.

Lucy rushed down the path and opened the shed door. For a moment she worried it had all been a dream, but then two white furry ears moved above the flowerpots and Starlight lifted his head to look at her. He was so beautiful.

Lucy could hardly believe that she was looking after a Christmas reindeer. This was the most important job she had ever had. She wouldn't let Santa down. He was relying on her.

"I can't stop, Starlight, but here's a carrot." Lucy put it down beside him. He stuck his little muzzle out to touch it, but didn't try to eat it.

"You must eat to get strong," Lucy said, and stroked his soft fur. His little tail started wagging, and he nudged her hand with his head, but he didn't try to get up. He was still very weak.

"Lucy!" Mom called from the kitchen. "Come and wash your hands and help me choose the cake decorations."

"I'm sorry, Starlight. I'll be back soon," Lucy said, tucking her dressing gown around him. "Please eat your carrot. I've got to get you better for Santa."

She put the velvet curtain down on top of a wheelbarrow. She hated leaving Starlight alone in the shed. What if someone looked through the window and saw him?

Starlight gave a little bleat.

"Ssh," Lucy said. "Mom's calling me so I've got to go. I'll put up that curtain later. Settle down and go to sleep. I'll be back as soon as I can."

Starlight
Gets Worse

As soon as Mom and Lucy had finished
decorating the cakes Lucy ran back to
the shed. Oscar and Dad would be back
soon and she didn't want either of them
to find Starlight.

He greeted her with a sweet little bleat and tried to get up, but he got tangled in her dressing gown and had to lie down again.

"No, Starlight," Lucy said firmly. "Stay there. I can't stop to stroke you. I've got to put this curtain up so nobody sees you. Mom says she won't come to the shed, but I don't want anyone looking through the window. I promised Santa I'd keep you secret."

Luckily, there must have been curtains in the shed before, because there was still an old curtain wire, so all Lucy had to do was hook the velvet curtain over it. The curtain was heavy and Lucy struggled to get it up, but she finally managed it. Now nobody could look in and see Starlight. It made the shed very dark, though.

"I'll be back in a minute," Lucy said. She could barely see Starlight in the dark, but he gave another little bleat. Lucy made her way to the sliver of daylight showing at the side of the shed door and came out into the winter sunshine. She ran back to the house and up to her room.

Lucy found what she was looking for. It was her night-light. She didn't really need it any more, but it was so pretty that sometimes she liked to keep it on at night and watch the snowflakes fall gently on the little house in the blue globe. She rushed back out to the shed with it.

"Look, Starlight. This will keep you company in the dark." She put it next to him and the gentle light lit up his fur and made his big eyes shine. He made a soft snickering sound and she really didn't want to leave him. Mom was right, the shed was very cold. That wouldn't help him get better.

Lucy tucked the dressing gown closer around him. He sniffed her hands gently, his ears twitching. He settled down and closed his eyes as the snowflakes in the glowing globe swirled around beside him. He looked thinner and weaker than he had been when they had woken up.

"I think Gran might have some little coats for the animals she rescues," Lucy said. "I'll go and see if she's in. I'll be back soon."

Lucy ran as fast as she could down the road and found Gran cleaning out the cages.

"A coat?" Gran said. "How big?"

Lucy stretched out her arms.

"That's big for a toy, Lucy."

"It's for Rocky," she stammered.

"Well, that one was for Monty, the little Shetland pony foal I had—why don't you try it?" Gran said, pointing to a bundle on the shelf.

"That's perfect!" Lucy said, relieved. It was soft and cozy. Starlight would love it.

"Lucy, is everything all right? You looked very worried for someone just playing a game," Gran said.

For a moment Lucy longed to tell Gran. "No. Everything is fine."

"Well, I'm here if you need me," Gran said, filling up the rabbit's water bowl.

"Water!" Lucy exclaimed. "I haven't given him water! I mean, I haven't pretended to give Rocky water!" And she rushed off back home.

Little Starlight was delighted to see her. She carefully put the soft coat on him, then the dressing gown back on top. He looked so sweet. He snuffled her face and tried to climb on to her lap.

"I've got to get you something to drink," Lucy said, gently pushing him off. She really wanted just to give him lots of hugs, but she had so much to do to get him well.

"What are you up to?" Oscar said from behind her as she filled a bowl with water from the kitchen sink.

"Nothing," Lucy said, and quickly poured it out again.

"Time for lunch, Lucy," Mom said, coming into the kitchen.

"Can I just—" began Lucy.

"No," said Mom. "I want us to have some nice family time and eat our lunch together. Come and sit down. Whatever you're doing can wait."

Lucy thought of little Starlight alone in the shed and hoped Mom was right. She tried to eat her baked potato and butter as quickly as possible. Luckily, Oscar and Dad were so busy telling Mom about the drum kit that nobody noticed that she had left a bit of baked potato in the bowl. She thought maybe Starlight might prefer it to the carrot.

When Mom and Dad and Oscar left the kitchen to go into the sitting room Lucy quickly got another bowl and filled it with water from the sink, and put both bowls on a tray to take down to the shed. Then she put on her boots, quietly opened the kitchen door, and crept out into the garden.

Poor Starlight didn't look at all well. He was lying flat on the sackcloths, completely exhausted. His white fur wasn't shining any more, and he looked thinner and his fur seemed paler than when she had left him. The night-light was still glowing, the snow still falling in the little globe.

"Starlight," Lucy said, kneeling down beside him. "Starlight, please get well. Please. Look, I've brought you some of my lunch, and some water." He raised his head to look at her, and his little tail gave a wag, but then he put his head down as if he was too tired.

"Caught you!" came a voice from behind her as a blast of cold air filled the shed. Lucy jumped and turned quickly to see Oscar standing in the doorway. "I knew you had an animal in the shed. I saw you take the carrot this morning, and then I saw you with the water bowl. I knew you were up to something!"

Oh no. Why did it have to be Oscar? "You mustn't tell anyone!" Lucy whispered urgently. "It's a reindeer. It's one of Santa's reindeer and Santa asked me to look after him and get him well for Christmas, but he's just getting worse," Lucy said.

Oscar walked in and looked past the line of flowerpots. When he saw what was in the shadows his mouth opened in surprise.

"Hey! Lucy! That's a deer. Where did you get him? You can't keep him in here."

"I know. I told you. It's one of Santa's reindeer," Lucy insisted.

"But Lucy, Santa—" Oscar started, but then stopped as Starlight lifted his head and looked straight into Oscar's astonished face. For a moment, the reindeer seemed to shimmer.

"What can we do?" Oscar said. He wasn't scornful anymore. He was kneeling down beside Starlight, stroking him gently, just as he used to do when he and Lucy both helped Gran with her animals.

"I don't know. I've given him food and water and a warm coat, but nothing has worked. But we have to do something, Oscar. It's Christmas Eve tomorrow!"

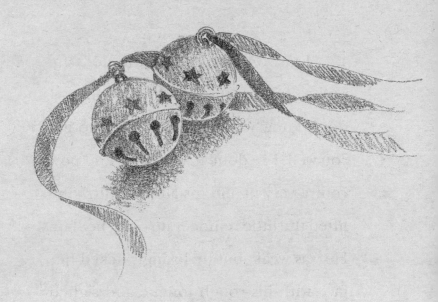

On the Mend

Starlight looked unwell, lying on the sackcloths in the back of the shed. His eyes were closed and he was panting. A tear ran down Lucy's cheek but she rubbed it angrily away.

"I just don't know what to do," she said to Oscar. "I'm so sorry, Starlight. I don't know why Santa chose me to get you well. I've done it all wrong, and now you're very ill and it's all my fault." She lifted the little reindeer up on to her lap. He was weak, but he lovingly licked her face with his rough tongue and sighed as he nestled down in her arms.

"Look, Lucy!" Oscar said suddenly.

There, in Lucy's arms, as she hugged him, the little reindeer stopped panting and sighed happily. His fur was getting whiter and brighter in front of their eyes and there was a soft light glowing all around him.

"Cuddling him is making him better!" Oscar said. "That's why Santa asked you, Lucy. He knows how good you are at hugs. Maybe Starlight just wasn't getting enough love and attention. You've kept him warm and given him food and water, but maybe on top of all those things, Christmas reindeer need love, and that's what's going to get him well."

It was true. Starlight's nose was getting blacker and shinier, and his tail was wagging more even as Lucy cuddled him. Maybe she could get him better after all. But there was still a problem.

"I can't stay here in the shed all day though," Lucy said.

"Why don't we smuggle him up to your bedroom?" Oscar suggested. "I'll go and tell Mom and Dad to stay out of the way. I'll tell them that I need to help you carry a special Christmas package up to your room."

Lucy and Oscar smuggled Starlight up to Lucy's room. Though he was small, he weighed too much for Lucy to carry him on her own, so together they carried him down the path wrapped up in a big soft bundle of rug and coats. His little nose stuck out and they were glad Mom and Dad had agreed to stay in the sitting room.

"Don't look, Mom and Dad!" Oscar called, as they came into the kitchen. Luckily, Starlight kept very calm as they struggled up the stairs, Oscar going up backwards and Lucy following. Starlight's big eyes blinked but he didn't make a sound, even when Lucy stumbled.

"Slow down!" Lucy said. "I nearly dropped him."

"Everything OK, kids?" Dad called. "Do you want any help?"

"No!" shouted Oscar and Lucy at the same time.

"Phew!" Oscar said, as they staggered into Lucy's bedroom and gently lay Starlight, in his bundle, on to the soft bed. He was very calm and sweet. They made a little nest for him with Lucy's pillows, and Rocky and Scruffy looked on. Oscar and Lucy looked at each other and laughed as Starlight wriggled around, making himself comfortable.

"He's amazing," Oscar said. Starlight snuffled and butted his head against Oscar's arm, lifting up his chin as if asking to be stroked. He was looking livelier already, and his fur was even

beginning to sparkle, although he didn't seem keen to get up and walk.

"I don't mind about getting presents any more—not even a kitten. I just want Starlight to get better," Lucy said, anxiously. "Do you think he'll be well enough to help Santa tomorrow?" she asked Oscar. They looked down at Starlight and he looked back and gave a little bleat.

They could hardly bear to leave Starlight to go down to dinner. Luckily, Dad and Mom were enjoying being together so much and were so busy chatting that they didn't notice Lucy and Oscar were never in the room at the same time.

"Can I say goodnight downstairs tonight?" Lucy asked at bedtime. "I've got a special Christmas surprise in my room and I don't want you to see it."

Mom and Dad laughed.

"OK, Lucy, we'll give you a hug down here then," Dad said.

"I'm looking forward to this Christmas surprise!" Mom said, giving Lucy a kiss. "Is it that puppet show you're making?"

"Not exactly," Lucy said. "Well, sort of. It's definitely Christmassy," she added and rushed upstairs before they asked her any more questions.

A Visit from Santa

Oscar came to give Starlight a last hug before he went to his room.

"Oscar, can you help me make the puppet show tomorrow?" Lucy asked. "I've got to cuddle Starlight."

"OK," Oscar said. "You're so lucky,"

he sighed. "I wish he was in my room. See you tomorrow, Starlight."

Lucy tried to get comfortable. It was definitely not easy sharing a bed with a little wriggly reindeer, no matter how soft and small he was. Finally, she decided to sit up, propped against her pillows. She would try to get him to settle down on her lap and go to sleep with his head resting on her arm.

"I'm going to hug you all night to get you better for tomorrow," Lucy said, before quickly falling fast asleep herself.

Lucy woke to the sound of sleigh bells jingling. Moonlight was streaming into her room where Starlight had pushed the curtains apart. He was standing on the bed, wide awake and bleating excitedly. His two front hooves were on the windowsill, and his little tail was wagging madly. His fur was gleaming white, his nose black and shiny. He looked completely well!

Lucy got out of bed, opened the curtains properly, and looked out of the window. She had to rub her eyes to check whether she was dreaming. There, in the night sky, was Santa! He was dressed all in red and was sitting in a beautiful silver sleigh, pulled by nine big brown reindeer. The reindeer snorted and stamped their hooves in the air, their breath forming lightly sparkling clouds.

"Thank you, Lucy!" Santa called above the sound of sleigh bells. "Starlight looks much better already!"

"What's going on?" came Oscar's sleepy voice. He was standing in the room, rubbing his eyes too. "I heard the sleigh bells and Starlight bleating, so I came to see what was happening."

Lucy pointed to the window, her mouth open in disbelief.

"Santa?" Oscar said in amazement.

"I can't believe it! You're in your sleigh and everything!"

Santa threw back his head and laughed, making Lucy and Oscar want to laugh too. "Yes, Oscar—I am! How about you and Lucy come for a ride?" Santa said. "Close your eyes and hold on to Starlight."

Lucy and Oscar put their hands on Starlight and closed their eyes tight. Suddenly they felt tingly and fizzy and bubbly with happiness. Something wonderful was happening! Before they knew it, sleigh bells tinkled again and they found themselves outside, sitting next to Santa in his sleigh up in the sky.

Little Starlight was on his knee, sitting up, bright and alert.

"Wow! This is AMAZING!" laughed Oscar, hugging Lucy in his excitement.

"I can't believe it!" Lucy said, looking over the edge of the sleigh, down at the garden and the shed. Normally, Lucy would have been frightened to be up so high, but being in Santa's sleigh felt like the safest and happiest place in the whole world.

"Take this blanket and keep warm," Santa said, tucking the blanket around their knees. His long white beard tickled Lucy as he leaned over. His red coat was soft and warm, and he smelled of cinnamon.

Starlight pointed his nose into the air, and the buds of his antlers began to glow, so that a tiny sparkling star appeared at the end of each one.

"Good boy, Starlight!" Santa laughed. "Now we won't get lost! Hold on tight, you two!" And he twitched the reins signaling to the reindeer to start flying.

Off they went, through the night sky, swooping over seas and cities and mountains, flying past the moon almost touching the stars, and seeing their shadows fall on the fields below. They were as fast as the wind, but with Santa beside them they didn't feel scared at all.

"We're just practicing for tomorrow!" Santa laughed, as they looked down on church steeples and forests, vast lakes, and busy cities twinkling with lights. "So many children waiting for their presents—we mustn't get it wrong!" he said, as they flew over castles and cottages in the countryside, and blocks of flats and rows of houses in towns.

Starlight sparkled in the night, never losing his balance, his muzzle pointing into the wind and his little ears twitching with excitement. Santa would tell him a place to go and then one of the stars on his antler buds twinkled and flashed to tell Santa whether to turn left or right. When they went straight on, his little nose sparkled, too.

"He's a reindeer SatNav!" Oscar laughed. "That's so cool!"

"So maybe when we see twinkling stars at night it's just Santa and Starlight planning their Christmas routes," Lucy said.

"Exactly!" Santa laughed. "We have to practice a lot to get it right for the big day. That's why Starlight is so important!"

It was all over too soon. Santa turned the sleigh around and they found themselves hovering in the air outside Lucy's room again. It seemed only minutes since the ride started, but they must have been out for much longer than that because the night sky was already getting lighter. It would soon be dawn.

"Well, this little fellow looks back to normal," Santa said, giving Starlight a pat. "He can't cope without his cuddles, and the elves have been so busy he has been fading away. I didn't think that he'd be ready for Christmas. But I knew you'd be able to make him better. I've got your Christmas letter safe and sound, by the way. Glad to see you wrote one in the end, Oscar!" Santa smiled at Oscar, his eyes twinkling.

Oscar blushed.

"And thanks for helping with Starlight. Christmas wouldn't be Christmas without my littlest reindeer. He points the way through the stars and finds the good in everyone."

Lucy looked at Oscar. He was smiling at Santa and stroking Starlight's head. It was true. Starlight and Santa saw that Oscar was still kind, deep down, even if he could be the grumpiest brother in the world at times.

"We'll say goodbye, now," Santa said. "We have a busy time ahead. It's dawn here but we still have the other side of the world to visit!"

Lucy flung her arms around Starlight. He gave her a loving lick.

"I don't want to leave him!" cried Lucy, but the next thing she knew, she was waking up in her bed. Scruffy was next to her, and Rocky was looking over at her with his kind eyes. But there was no little reindeer.

Missing Starlight

Lucy ran out of her bedroom and met Oscar on the landing. They looked at each other.

"Did you have a dream about—" they both said at the same time, and then stopped.

"So it *was* true then," Oscar said. "Starlight and the sleigh and Santa. Everything! Wow."

"Yes," Lucy said. "It's more wonderful than I could ever have imagined. It's the best thing that has ever happened. Ever. I just wish we could have kept Starlight here. He's so sweet."

"He'll be happier with Santa," Oscar said. "And Santa needs him—imagine all the children who wouldn't get presents if Starlight didn't guide the sleigh to their homes. Come on, Lucy, cheer up! Race you down to breakfast."

"Who wants pancakes?" Dad asked cheerfully as they came into the kitchen. "I've got a feeling this is going to be one of our best Christmases yet!" he said, getting out the frying pan.

Then his mobile phone rang.

"It's work," he said, surprised. "What are they doing, calling me on Christmas Eve?" He picked it up, and then his face became very serious.

"Yes. Hello. Yes, I can talk now. Wait a minute, I'll take the phone into the next room."

"Carry on without me," he mouthed to Mom, and walked out of the kitchen.

Lucy and Oscar looked at each other. Why was Dad's work calling him at Christmas?

They didn't have long to wait. Dad came back into the kitchen, a huge smile on his face. He went over to Mom and gave her a big hug, picking her up and whirling her round.

"You'll never guess! You remember I applied for that manager's job? More money and based locally? They have just called to tell me I've got it! I start in the New Year! I won't have to travel away from home anymore!"

"I can't believe it!" Mom said. "That's wonderful news!"

Everyone was so happy they didn't notice Lucy slipping away upstairs.

"I'm really glad Dad has a new job and we can all be together again," she said to Scruffy and Rocky. "But I miss Starlight so much. It's all I can think about. It was so special looking after him."

There was a knock on the door.

"Are you OK, Lucy?" Mom asked.

"Yes, just a bit tired, that's all," Lucy replied.

"Well, Dad says he wants to take us all out for lunch to celebrate, and then this afternoon I thought we could finish decorating the tree and maybe cuddle up and watch a film together? Dad and Gran and Oscar have to go out to do some special Christmas shopping now . . . Oh, I'm so happy, Lucy! I can't believe we're going to have Dad around at home again!" Mom gave Lucy a big hug, and Lucy could hear her singing as she went back downstairs.

"Thank you, Santa, for asking me to help make Starlight better," Lucy said, once she was on her own. "I'm sorry I'm not more happy. I will try." She cuddled Scruffy and tried to be brave. Rocky seemed to rock a little, as if to say he understood.

"At least I have you two," Lucy sighed.

The rest of the day was so busy that even though Lucy still had an ache inside from missing Starlight, she didn't really have time to be too sad. After a lovely lunch they came home to get on with getting ready for Christmas Day. Decorating the Christmas tree was always one of Lucy's favorite things to do. It was fun to find the Christmas fairy and put her back on top of the tree, and Dad and Mom kept talking about the new job.

Then the packages started appearing at the bottom of the tree. Gran came over with lots, including

a huge flat one and two smaller ones for Lucy. Upstairs, Lucy wrapped up a jewelry box she had made for Mom, a mug she had painted with "Best Dad Ever!" on for Dad, a brooch with a badger on it for Gran, and a book of jokes for Oscar.

Before long, it was dark. They all wrapped up warm and went to hear the Christmas carols in town. They ate hot chestnuts as the brass band played. Little flakes of snow drifted down and the lights in the shop fronts twinkled. It was magical.

"This is the best Christmas ever!" Oscar said.

If only we still had Starlight, Lucy thought, but she didn't say anything.

The Best Christmas Day Ever

Lucy woke up to the sound of loud drumming.

"Put the headphones on, Oscar!" Dad shouted, but he didn't sound too cross.

Remembering that it was Christmas Day, Lucy quickly opened her eyes. Her stocking at the end of the bed was bulging! There was a long shape wrapped in colorful paper poking out of the top, and when she held the toe of the stocking, she could feel lots of hard little flat round shapes. Chocolate coins! And a new red pencil case with her name on it in gold swirly letters! Inside the case there were beautiful colored pens with her name in gold on each of them, too. Lucy ate two chocolate coins and smiled as she thought of how Starlight must've been well enough to guide Santa to her house in the night.

She tried not to be sad that he hadn't been able to stay and see her open her presents.

Oscar was eventually persuaded off the drums and they all had a special Christmas breakfast together. There were scrambled eggs and thick slices of warm, buttered toast, and Mom had made freshly squeezed orange juice. Mom was really happy with the decorated box Lucy had made for her, and Dad loved his painted mug.

"I'll have my Christmas tea in it!" Dad said, beaming.

"Thank you so much, Lucy!" Mom said. "What a lovely surprise! No wonder you were so mysterious and busy yesterday!" Lucy squirmed a little, and didn't say that she had made the gifts at school.

Lucy was given a smart new watch from Mom and Dad, and a false mustache set from Oscar. They were all trying on mustaches and laughing when the doorbell rang. Mom and Dad looked at each other and smiled.

"Go and answer that, Lucy," Dad said.

Excited, Lucy went to open the door.

"Hello, Lucy! Happy Christmas, darling!" Gran said, hugging her with one arm because the other was holding a big wicker basket.

When Gran and Lucy came into the sitting room Oscar and Dad and Mom were standing in front of the Christmas tree, smiling.

"Have you given it to her yet?" Oscar asked Gran.

"No," Gran said, laughing. She passed the basket to Dad, who carefully put it down.

"Lucy, come and open the lid," said Mom. "Whatever is inside is for you!"

Lucy opened it and looked inside. There was something small and ginger and furry—she couldn't believe it! Carefully she reached inside and brought out . . . a tiny little kitten! It had big blue eyes, a little pink nose, and soft fluffy fur.

"Oh!" Lucy said. "She's beautiful!"

"She's yours," Dad said. "Because you are such a kind girl. We can't think of anyone better to look after her." Lucy couldn't stop smiling. Santa had made her wish come true!

The rest of Christmas Day was the happiest day Lucy could remember. Mom and Dad made a delicious Christmas lunch with all the trimmings. Oscar (with his headphones on) played the drums, and Gran and Lucy played with the little kitten. At first she was shy, and cuddled up on Lucy's lap, watching everyone with her big kitten eyes. But soon she began to explore, and then decided that Christmas was the most fun ever. She chased ribbons and even tried to climb the tree! After lunch, she jumped on the Christmas paper as Lucy unwrapped the big flat package from Gran.

"It's a puppet theater! Thanks, Gran!" Lucy said. "You can have your velvet curtain back, Mom. I didn't have time to use it to make my own theater, and now I don't need it. Look what Gran got me!"

It was beautiful—painted red and gold and made of three sections which stood up when unfolded with a red velvet curtain for the background. But the puppets were even better. They were beautifully painted wooden stick puppets—one of Santa and his silver sleigh being pulled by nine reindeer, and then one tiny little reindeer puppet on its own.

"How unusual!" Mom said, admiring them. "Wherever did you get them?" she asked Gran.

"From a very special workshop," Gran replied, and smiled at Oscar and Lucy. "This little reindeer is very sweet. I wonder what his name is. It can't be Rudolph because there's already one with a red nose pulling the sleigh."

"It's Starlight," Lucy said, looking down at the little puppet, and she and Oscar smiled at each other. They knew exactly what their puppet show would be about.

"And what are you going to call this little one?" Mom asked.

The kitten jumped off Lucy's lap and rushed around the room, pouncing on stray bits of Christmas paper and leaping up on to the drums and down again. Everyone laughed. She was a totally gorgeous, completely mad ball of fluff.

"Merry!" Lucy said. "Because this really is a merry Christmas!"

At the end of what had been a very happy Christmas Day, Oscar reluctantly left his drum kit and went to bed with his joke book, and Gran went home to feed the animals. Merry the kitten had played herself to sleep, curled up next to Scruffy, warm and snug on Lucy's bed.

"I can't believe you're here," Lucy marveled, stroking her sleepily. It was certainly easier to cuddle a kitten than a reindeer. "Thank you, Santa. I hope Starlight isn't too tired after his big day."

Soon after, Mom and Dad came to kiss her goodnight.

"Sleep well, Lucy. Sleep well, Merry." Mom laughed as the kitten stretched out her little legs. She looked as happy and relaxed as Mom and Dad did. "I loved your puppet show about the reindeer Starlight who needed to get well for Christmas," Mom said.

"Sweet dreams, lovely Lucy," Dad said, as he kissed her. "It's been a great Christmas, hasn't it? All our wishes have come true!" He blew her another kiss as he pulled the door closed behind them.

"Goodnight, Rocky, goodnight, Scruffy, goodnight, Merry," Lucy said. She looked at the softly-glowing night-light

beside her bed, with the snowflakes
falling on the little house. For a
moment, she thought the door of
the house opened and a small figure,
dressed in red, came out, with a tiny
white deer running excitedly around
in circles at his feet. He looked up at
her and waved. She rubbed her eyes
and looked again,
but if there
had been

anything there, it was gone. No Santa, no reindeer, just snow falling on a little house in the woods. Yet Lucy smiled as she remembered the sleigh ride, and the softness of Starlight's fur, and how Santa had smelled of cinnamon.

"Goodnight Santa, goodnight Starlight—wherever you both are! Happy Christmas, and thank you!" Lucy whispered. And, kissing Merry on top of her warm little head, Lucy settled down to go to sleep.

About the author

Every Christmas, Anne used to ask for a dog. She had to wait many years, but now she has two dogs, called Timmy and Ben. Timmy is a big, gentle golden retriever who loves people and food and is scared of cats. Ben is a small brown and white cavalier King Charles spaniel who is a bit like a cat because he curls up in the warmest places and bosses Timmy about. He snuffles and snorts quite a lot and you can tell what he is feeling by the way he walks. He has a particularly pleased patter when he has stolen something he shouldn't have, which gives him away immediately. Anne also has two hens called Anastasia and Poppy. Anne lives in a village in Kent and is not afraid of spiders.